Crick and Crock Have Lunch

Written by Susan Frame

Illustrated by Marcela Calderón

Collins

Crick the crab picks up her
silver lunchbox.

She slips into a crack in the rocks.

Crick lifts up the lid of her lunchbox.

Then, she has a quick sniff.

sniff
sniff

Crick picks up a kelp sandwich.

There is no drink in her lunchbox.

Crick hears a soft tap on the rock.

"It's Crock," thinks Crick.

Come and join me, Crock.

Next, Crock lifts the lid of
her lunchbox.

Crock has a milk drink.

"Here is some sandwich for you," grins Crick.

"Have some milk," grins Crock.

Lunch

Letters and Sounds: Phase 4

Word count: 100

Focus on adjacent consonants with short vowel phonemes, e.g. *drink*.

Common exception words: have, the, she, into, of, no, come, me, here, some, you, what, there, I

Curriculum links (EYFS): Understanding the world; PSED: Making relationships

Curriculum links (National Curriculum, Year 1): Science: Animals, including humans; PSHE: Health and wellbeing

Early learning goals: Reading: read and understand simple sentences; use phonic knowledge to decode regular words and read them aloud accurately; read some common irregular words; demonstrate understanding when talking with others about what they have read

National Curriculum learning objectives: Reading/word reading: read accurately by blending sounds in unfamiliar words containing GPCs that have been taught; Reading/comprehension: understand both the books they can already read accurately and fluently and those they listen to by checking that the text makes sense to them as they read, and correcting inaccurate reading; making inferences on the basis of what is being said and done

Developing fluency

- Encourage your child to follow the words as you read the first pages with expression.
- Read the narrator's words and encourage your child to read the thought and spoken words, including the words in the speech bubbles. Ask your child to make the characters' voices sound interesting and real.

Phonic practice

- Model sound talking the word **grins** (g-r-i-n-s). Encourage your child to sound talk the following with you:

  lifts   lunch   drink   milk

- Challenge your child to sound talk the following words with more than one syllable, breaking them into chunks to help:

  silver   lunchbox   sandwich

Extending vocabulary

- Ask your child to look at the pictures and think of a word for how Crick or Crock might be feeling.

  page 5 e.g. *hungry, curious*   page 7 e.g. *disappointed, sad*